The Arab King
of
My Heart and Soul

Far East Meets Middle East

Yuriko Terasaka

authorHOUSE®

AuthorHouse™
1663 Liberty Drive
Bloomington, IN 47403
www.authorhouse.com
Phone: 1 (800) 839-8640

Published by AuthorHouse 12/28/2016

ISBN: 978-1-5246-5638-6 (sc)
ISBN: 978-1-5246-5639-3 (hc)
ISBN: 978-1-5246-5637-9 (e)

Library of Congress Control Number: 2016921073

Print information available on the last page.

To my mother, Ikuko Terasaka Moore, and my father, Ernest Dean Moore. Without them, I would not exist.

Foreword

Physical attractions are very common. Mental connections are very rare. And soul connections are priceless.

Everything is better with a king. My heart was closed, and little did I know the Arab king held the key in his palm. The world is our kingdom, and the region is my heart. I ponder the space between his fingers. Could my fingers fit there perfectly? I imagine the feel of his arms holding me, my armor. The beauty of the soul is love without the eyes.

Social media has certainly revolutionized relationship building across all generations. I feel it is important to use the benefits of these technologies to acquire knowledge of other cultures for human connections. People can easily find commonality by what they share on social media. Travels, food, entertainment, hobbies, everything is a posting. Therefore, the ubiquity of social media can pinpoint a match.

Virtual relationships can cornerstones for some. They can enhance lives and lead to valuable, long-lasting commitments.

Affection: It is not possible to have an actual hug, kiss, or physical touch with a virtual relationship. There are many icons, apps, and words to express your affection. And these can be just as warmly felt as being physically touched.

Respect: Social media is the perfect platform for expressing proud accomplishments, appreciation, congratulations, or admiration. Taking time to listen and convey our thoughts is crucial.

Support: Social media can give and receive the support we need easily. Doing acts of kindness and providing advice is crucial in all relationships.

Quality time: Social media access is 24-7. You can spend unlimited time during different time zones easily. Quality time is necessary for relationships. Social media provides that degree of excellence.

Social media is an aid for connecting one another in a thorough and extensive manner, which is of paramount importance.

The Arab King of My Heart and Soul is the accumulation of all the social media tools offered. There is an exchange of power. I am his weakness, and he is my strength. True love is not about the person. It is a beautiful treasure. When two souls recognize each other, they honor that love, light, beauty, truth, and kindness. There is no difference, no distance. They are one in the same. Love is understood by all cultures, yet it is the heart that understands completely for unification. Will his heart answer the call of mine? Can I entrust him with the most fragile part of me?

The thought of his nearness takes my breath away. Without our communication, there is no relationship. Without respect, there is no love, and without trust, there is no reason to continue. With my soul, I can see his handsome face, feel his touch, even though *The King of My Heart and Soul* is intangible.

My Face Will Fade

Mashalany is the conductor of my heart and soul, and the music has reached a crescendo.

True beauty is shown by the heart and soul, which will go on forever.

I can feel his power, his dominance pulling me closer to him. His force is so strong I can't leave or ignore the energy he exudes. I don't need to be in his physical presence to feel his vivacity. When I hear his voice, it takes me higher to infinity. If he were standing in front of me with his arms around me, I feel like we would burn like fire from the electricity. The smoldering flame of passion will not go out.

Mashalany touches the edges of my soul, which have been hidden from the world until now. In the darkness he is real, yet he seems no more real in my dreams. Will he give me his heart?

I feel we are in a real romance. Our hearts are touching, and our souls are emphasized. His courtesies are small and trivial, yet they strike deep into my grateful and appreciative heart. His eyes never request permission to see me on Skype or Facetime. He acknowledges my passion and affection. We have a spiritual and virtual relationship, which makes our hearts and souls complete. He doesn't seem to care for the outside beauty, only my inner beauty.

A Glimpse of Paradise

Love is a strong feeling that captures the heart, mind, and soul and makes you crave for that special someone's presence in each moment of your life. Love is when you see the world through their eyes. Love is where you find peace in their arms. It is when you feel you can connect with someone physically, emotionally, mentally, and soulfully all at the same time. Love is when you take care of the feelings, the emotions, and the emotional needs of the one you love. It is when you are madly, crazily, and insanely in love with every inch of another's body, mind, heart, and soul all at the same time. Love is not just about sexual intimacy but the feeling of emotional, soulful, and spiritual intimacy between two people who can feel the passion all the way through their hearts and souls.

When the heart and soul are engaged, magic happens—an illumination of complete love and true happiness. No hormones are involved because there is no physical presence—only words shared through feelings and music. You can find solace in music without the presence of another. Music, which has often been called the most abstract of the arts, is in the historical sense the most concrete, for art is more integrally related to the dimension of time. The composition is itself history. The sense of each transient note both determines and is determined by that which has been and that which will come. Musical sound unfolds in a continuous, transitory present. Music heals the heart and opens the heart and soul.

Too many people love with their eyes and not with the heart. You can't control what your heart feels and sees. Platonic love is two bodies and one soul. The animalistic desire based on lust can be superseded by the more intellectual conception of love. Physical desires share commonality with the animal kingdom, which is the lowest form of love. The true beauty of real love is not the physical form. Love produced by an exploration of ideas defines the true pursuit of the beauty in love. To be a heart and soul troubadour, the desire for the physical must not be of significant importance. Even with the knights and damsels, their true love was not consummated; the knights pursued chivalric deeds instead of sensual pursuits. This puts the heart and soul at a much higher level. Sexual gratification is the lowest form of love. The recognition of another soul completes one's own soul; it complements each soul.

There is a clear distinction between love and romantic love. Romantic love is all about the surface, the physical. Love is about the heart and soul. It's about kindness, and it is long-lasting, respectful, and passionate. The heart and soul develop kindness unmasked, and they do not proclaim the act complete.

True connections of the spirit require no words. There is simply knowing.

On average most relationships begin with 70 percent body language. Mashalany and I have no body language. We have only the tone of our voices and content of each message. We do not have the luxury of a soft touch of the hand or a gentle tilt of his head or even a blink of his eye or the comfort of a smile.

I now understand why it doesn't work with others without the souls engaged and why Mashalany deserves my heart.

The spirit of true love is without condition. It's talk without intention. It's giving without reason and caring without expectation.

True love is found with the heart and soul, not the eyes. The heart will glow and lead. Furthermore, in the end we won't remember the beauty of our bodies, only the beauty of our hearts and souls. We see clearly with our hearts. What is essential is invisible to the eyes.

Our way was unplanned, and our path was unknown; however, our journey was made as one. I ponder the thought of his touch like a flower hugging another flower.

I don't want to define love because this love is more beautiful than any meaning we could construe.

No Damsel in Distress

I am a woman who embraces my femininity and all my womanhood with great passion. I adore being a woman, for we inspire the whole world. The beauty each of us has within us is not found in our physical attributes. I am not a damsel in distress looking for her king. I'm a strong woman with capabilities of my own. All the stories we have to share, none of us has an easy life on earth, so each of us has an incredible journey to share. This is one story I am proud to share because it changed my life, and my hope is that you, too, will receive some benefit for your journey in finding total and complete love.

Beauty doesn't make love; however, love makes beauty. Break anything but never break a heart, for the heart is the music played beautifully. Never play with the heart. I truly believe that to love is the will to live, and a heart that truly loves stays forever young. True love is without demands, and it does not ask for anything in return.

I am a normal woman who seeks a man who is unique to my heart and soul, who speaks to my very being. Rare is the ability to have eyes only for you, hands only to pray for you, a mind to care only for you, and a heart only for you. Give laughter to all, a smile only to you, a cheek for all, lips only for you, love to all, the heart only to you, and allow everyone to love him. But his love is only for you. I am never separated because he lives in my heart and soul.

I share my fairy tale with you in a unique, powerful, and most unusual encounter with my Arabian king of my heart and soul.

Love Is Being a Woman

Mashalany respects and appreciates that I am a strong woman, and he doesn't expect me to appear weak just so he looks strong.

I'm a professional woman who must maintain a certain seriousness on a daily basis. As a Japanese-American woman, this also adds a certain spin to the way I look at life. We all arrived on earth the exact same way, and we all leave earth the exact same way—no difference. The only difference is the way we look and our environments. I have the curiosity of a cat, and I'm probably on the ninth life! I want to travel the world and see everyone in their own world and how they cope with everyday life. I will be a sponge for their energy, inspiration, fortitude, perseverance, struggles, and each their own beauty.

I am proud to be born a female, unique and confident about showing the world my true character. I love who I am, my body that was given to me, and I'm grateful for how it works for me.

I welcome the inspiration of others, and I only surround myself with authentic and organic people. I possess my own talents, inspiration, and appreciate the entire world of beauty and awe. I can no longer be bored because life is just too unbelievable.

I am virtuous, valuable, valued, vibrant, and vivacious!

There seems to be a fascination with Japanese women around the world. Perhaps it because of the mystic of geisha? Or anime? I must first clarify a few ideologies about Japanese women. We are not *easy* or *whores*. This is the first big misconception. If you are not Japanese, it is difficult to understand the geisha. The Japanese are proud of the geisha tradition. Geishas are truly talented and trained for making music, writing poetry, playing traditional Japanese instruments, singing, dancing, sharing proper conversations, and maintaining etiquette. You would never see any open indiscretions. Any impurities would not be openly known. A geisha is not comparable to a hooker, prostitute, or call girl. If you were to visit Kyoto today, you would see many geishas. If you look close, you can tell the fake from the true geisha. First, you will never see a true geisha stop for photos. Of course, geishas know they are a novelty. However, they are very busy, and they will not stop until they reached their destination. Geishas have a very long history in Japan, and their role has changed with time. *Gei* means artist in Japanese. They are truly artistic in each move they make—from their voice to their actions.

The beauty of the geisha is seen through her eyes and the entrance to her heart. I feel like the geisha with mystery, sharing the same honesty, intelligence, courageous heart, confidence, compassion, independence, strength, and grace, as we are no ordinary women. We are quiet in spirit yet seen for our good hearts.

I'm not the most beautiful woman in the world. Nevertheless, I want to make Mashalany's world beautiful. Lust is the empty feeling of the physical. I want to wake up to Mashalany every beautiful morning.

Mashalany does not expect me to be a supermodel or high-level executive. It has more do with what is unseen or the admiration for each other. We plant the seeds of what is concealed for a magnificent result. Synthetic relationships cannot be long term. There is a resounding effort from both of us. Each one puts in a 100 percent for a forever friendship, which creates a positive flow. The open communication between us is key—no pride or ego, just simple honest communication. We are able to live in the moment and give undivided attention, and with each encounter, the words penetrate more deeply. Building a respectable and long-term relationship takes commitment and hard work when you can't be in the physical presence. It takes ingenuity, cleverness, strength, unusual cultivation, time, and extraordinary patience. It would be easy to drift apart without our exceptional passion.

In my daily life of analyzing, I find relief in not having to analyze and pick apart our relationship. Neither one of us is perfect. And we acknowledge that nothing is absolutely perfect on earth.

Mashalany is able to make me laugh and think twice about life. I accept the fact he does not think of me each moment of the day. He has the part of me that he can break at any moment. I have no desire to change him, hurt him, or expect more than he can give me. I accept him as he is. I glorify in the moments he provides for a smile, laugh, or education, and of course, I miss him daily. Our circumstance is not for everyone, yet we have construed a relationship for envy.

Only once in your lifetime will you truly find someone who will take your world upside down. I can tell Mashalany things that I've never shared with another soul, and he absorbs everything I say and actually wants to hear more. I share hopes for the future, dreams that may never come true, goals that may never be achieved, and the many disappointments life has thrown at us. When something wonderful happens, I can't wait to tell him about it, knowing he will share in my excitement. I am not embarrassed to cry with him when I am hurting or laugh with him when I make a fool of myself. Mashalany never hurts my feelings or makes me feel like I am not good enough, but he builds me up and shows me the things about myself that make me special and even beautiful. There is never any pressure, jealousy, or competition but only a quiet calmness when he speaks to me. I can be myself and not worry about what he will think of me because he gives me credence for who I am. The things that seem insignificant to other people, such as a note or song, become invaluable treasures kept safe in my heart to cherish forever. Mashalany makes me feel young again. Colors seem brighter and more brilliant. Laughter seems part of daily life when before it was infrequent or didn't exist at all. A message or two during the day helps me get you through a long day's work and always brings a smile to my face. There's no need for continuous conversation; however, I find I'm quite content in just having him in my heart. Things that never interested me before become fascinating because I know they are important or special to Mashalany. I think of him on every occasion and in everything I do. Simple things bring him to mind like a pale blue sky, a gentle wind, or even a storm cloud on the horizon. I have my heart open, knowing that there's a chance it may be broken one day, and in opening my heart, I experienced a love and joy that I never dreamed possible. I find that being vulnerable is the only way to allow my heart to feel true pleasure that's so real it scares me at times. I find strength in knowing I have a true friend and a soul mate who will remain loyal to the end. Life seems completely different, exciting, and worthwhile. My only hope and security is in knowing that he is a part of my life.

I can only offer love that is unfiltered; a love that is independent, inquisitive, fearless, caring, open, stellar, unbroken, and ready; a love worthy of beautiful magic and power beyond our imagination. This love is revolutionary and authentic, and it should be shared.

Haiku

Haiku is Japanese poetry that usually depicts the natural world and often focuses on the elements of love and sensuality. Haiku is an elegant anthology of love expressed in the feelings of the heart, the vision of love, and the poignant moments that express it.

Mashalany is a haiku for this century. He did a million things he never knew he was doing.

There are some similarities with my story of the Arab king from Palestine and the Japanese culture. The Japanese people grew up with the principles of bushido, a Japanese warrior. Being seen with women prior to marriage is strictly prohibited. Even speaking in public is strictly prohibited. However, once they are married and children, Japanese men are like the bushido—very protective. And Japanese families maintain themselves with very little divorce or domestic violence, which is not so true of Western cultures.

Most Japanese men will not ask women out unless they are thinking about marriage. Moreover, most Japanese men are timid and actually afraid that the women they love will reject their proposals. Japanese men also avoid beautiful and adorable women. *Takane no hana* translates as "Beautiful flower grows on steep mountain." In other words, they are hard to acquire. I believe women should all be hard to acquire.

Haiku love is a spiritual voyage toward two souls into one. With Mashalany we have a total sharing of feelings, emotions, and sensations in a deep way. We are truly engaged emotionally with genuine interest and caring without the intimacy.

We both place great value in each of our families. Our interactions are value based for caring for each other, at the same time we are completely open.

Mashalany is the very substance and material dreams are made of.

We wake up the Butterfly, so much to do, see, and accomplish.

Heart-minded we harmonize as one beat for the power of a beautiful love. Ear-to-Soul is all we need to go on. Our souls are timeless, eternal, infinitely wise susurrations prudent insights into our ears.

"Give Mashalany a try," my heart whispered and so I did.

I Am Japanese Woman

I relate to these the classical Heian period, which offers the earliest full-length forms of women's writing known in the globe. I am the woman they write about. The fact is so striking as to why modern readers must endeavor to discover why and how women wrote, what sociopolitical circumstances enabled their literary production. Clearly, women authors like Sei Shônagon and Murasaki Shikibu were highly educated, which leads us to reflect upon the important role of the education of Japanese women and their achievements. We must ask why, considering that it has not always been a priority in premodern world history, it was considered important for Japanese women in the Heian period. Since these women authors were members of the court aristocracy (albeit the middle or lower-middle rungs of it), should we conclude that social class was a dominant enabling factor for their writing? Literacy, the ability to read and write, has ever been a prerequisite for respectable membership in the upper classes in East Asia.

The situation for Heian women's education was also influenced by gender difference and segregation. Women of the aristocracy were kept away from the public gaze after puberty and even after marriage. The only males allowed to see them directly were their fathers, husbands, and children. Lovers in illicit relationships could only come at night, which did not guarantee they would see one another. This is not to say that women had no social life, only that male visitors were required to converse with them through a portable wood-framed barrier of curtain panels.

Did the fact of gender segregation encourage the apparent promiscuity of letters and poems exchanged between the sexes and the plot of the Heian love story, which inevitably begins with the stolen glimpse of a lady as the inciting force? Again, it is striking to note that there are no very explicit descriptions of women's faces and bodies in Heian writing. Not even from the women writers themselves, who resided in close quarters with other women at court. On the contrary, it is the breeding, education, cultural training, sensitivity, and character revealed by a woman's speech, writing, poetry, music, behavior, and so on that are used to describe her—all the inner beauty qualifications. The physical is not important.

In this segregated milieu, a woman's identity was a construct, an effect of her culture as filtered through her correspondence and other people's impressions of her. Thus, writing was a woman's vital link to others outside her immediate circle. Where she was not seen, she could be heard or read.

Much has been made of the Heian gender difference in education. Males were formally schooled in the academy (Daigaku) with a curriculum consisting of the Chinese classics in the fields of philosophy, ethics, ritual, and letters or literature, including poetry and history. Females did not need such schooling, but they had to be proficient in Japanese (as distinct from Chinese) writing and reading, poetry, and music. Were women deprived of opportunities because of their confinement to the sphere of the Japanese language? Would their minds and their writing have expanded had they been trained in the Chinese classics?

Here we must consider that intellectually curious women like Murasaki Shikibu did not allow social and gender conventions to keep them from reading Chinese. This is clear from her writing. Yet we must ask how even richer Heian writing would have been had women been schooled, as a matter of course, in the philosophical and ethical issues raised in the Chinese classics—and more to the point, how their social position would have been legitimized by such schooling. The ambivalence with which learning (i.e., Chinese learning) for a woman was viewed is evident in Murasaki's comic depiction of it in one of the excerpts here.

And finally, is it not one of the ironic effects of history that it was the women, deprived of a formal Chinese education, who pioneered what would later be recognized as the distinctly Japanese literary tradition? And in their concern for the private and personal—family and kinship ties, love relationships, the details of a lived life, self-introspection—women produced such revealing portraits of an age so far removed from ours yet so close in their similar concerns.

In what way do questions raised by Sei Shônagon in her *Pillowbook* indicate a proto-feminist attitude? For example, analyze her defense of service at court as lady-in-waiting, which may be considered a career for the upper- and middle-class women of the Heian period. What does she see as its advantages over the ordinary role of housewife? Consider also Sei's admiration for high office and apparent envy of the fact that almost all offices were reserved for males. Note her apparent pride in the praise her poetry receives from some male courtiers and their inability to top off her lines. Do her attitudes reveal an awareness of the weak position of women in Heian society and a desire for greater gender equality?

One of the many reasons why the Heian period is important for Japanese cultural history is because its poetry, collected in the court-commissioned anthology *Kokin Wakashu* (compiled ca. 905 CE), became the model for poetic forms and themes in all the subsequent centuries. The most distinctive characteristic of Heian poetry is that in it, nature becomes a language, at once vast and minute, for the expression of human feeling. And it is this poetic sensibility, which is assimilated into the prose descriptions and narratives of women's writing, that becomes associated with a distinctively Japanese literature. Sharpen students' understanding of the women writers' attitude to nature by articulating how time is of the essence in this awareness, how it is the temporal perspective that is the basis of evocations of light, color, temperature, tactility, among others in Sei's nature descriptions—time grasped as the succession of the seasons, or as the hour of the day and its changing atmospheric manifestations in natural phenomena and places. Speculate on how the possession of such an awareness can become, as it did become, a kind of index of one's membership in a certain class and later of one's belonging to a certain people, the Japanese.

Is it feasible to discuss female desire on the basis of women's writing? Reflect on whether or not women—whether in the Heian period or other times and places before our own—are free to explicitly reveal their desires. Might Sei Shônagon be exceptional in her candid (some would say opinionated) expression of her likes and dislikes? When it comes to love, a theme commonly associated with women's writing, does she seem more interested in the way it is conducted rather than the sincerity of feeling? Or is it precisely the way the lover behaves that indicates his seriousness? Is courtesy, the observation of etiquette and good manners, as important as unadulterated feeling? Why? Is it possible that ritual and etiquette are more advantageous for women than not? Given her sense of gender rivalry, is Sei perhaps more interested in the power balance (or imbalance) in gender relations than in questions of love? Is desire for recognition of one's authority an acceptable female desire?

The *Tale of Genji* thematizes in great detail what men desire in women early on in the novel. Read the section called "Rainy Night Disquisition on the Types of Women." In discussing this section, it is important to note that the point of view represented is solely male since there is not a single female participant in the conversation—except, that is, for the author-narrator, the woman writer representing the male, which one may assume is the orthodox view. Thus, it is useful to adopt a certain irony when reading this passage and to point out in what way this irony, though very subtle, is indicated. If one reads *Genji* itself, it will be evident that the female characteristics laid out here are foregrounded in the subsequent stories of various heroines and that there is an implicit protest against the objectification of women by typecasting them in this way. Would it be fair to say that the men reveal their egoism in considering only their own desires and not that of the women as well? We can articulate the logical relation between male authority, whether verbal or sociopolitical, and female self-denial.

Use the excerpt from the *Sarashina Diary* to discuss the apparent attraction, even seductiveness, of women-authored fiction and stories evoking the feminine imaginary as against the moral, didactic stories in religious literature like the *Lotus Sutra*. Read the fifth volume of the sutra to discover how the female body is represented in one of the major Buddhist canonical texts. Consider Heian women's writing as *subaltern* literature in relation to the Confucian and Buddhist canons.

Analyze the reasons for the ambivalence some women apparently felt about Chinese learning based on the excerpts from *The Tale of Genji* and the *Murasaki Shikibu Diary*. Note the existence of a hierarchical gender difference in writing. Chinese writing was considered male and learned, and Japanese writing female and graceful. Consider Murasaki Shikibu's discomfort with becoming the subject of gossip because of her interest in the Chinese classics within the context of this ideological gender divide. Relate that to the comic/parodic treatment of the learned woman in *Genji* and Murasaki's anecdote in the *Diary* about her early proficiency in the Chinese classics compared to her brother.

What are the disadvantages (from a woman's perspective) of the Heian marriage practice of polygamy (*ippu tazai*, meaning one husband to many wives) or polygyny? Speculate on why jealousy or sexual anger seems to be considered the gravest fault in a woman. In reading the excerpt about Lady Rokujô in *Genji*, note how the author delves into Rokujô's psychology of mingled pride and shame, the public loss of dignity she suffers as the widow of a crown prince in love with Genji, who is married to another woman, Aoi, and has no apparent intentions of making Rokujô one of his wives. This can be related to Muslim men, who are allowed to take four wives. Sometimes I feel the same as Lady Rokujô in *Genji*. I will not be part of Mashalany's court. I'm only allowed to peer into his courtships.

Fleeting Beauty of Cherry Blossoms

Are we to look at cherry blossoms only in full bloom, the moon only when it is cloudless? To long for the moon while looking on the rain, to lower the blinds and be unaware of the passing of spring—these are even more deeply moving. Branches about to bloom or gardens strewn with faded flowers are worthier of our admiration—in all things, it is the beginnings and endings that are interesting ... If man were never to fade away but lingered on forever in the world, how things would lose their power to move us. The most precious thing in life is its uncertainty.

—Yoshida Kenko

Japanese take daily time to appreciate the beauty of nature. Life is fragile just as the cherry blossoms. An errant breeze can take away the cherry blossom. Life is precious in all of these moments.

In Asian cultures, cherry blossom meanings usually include brave, industrious, and wise. The cherry blossom is fundamentally a symbol of love and joy. It is believed that the cherry blossom promotes love and spiritual awareness. The sakura trees in Japan are highly esteemed. Japan's samurai culture admired the cherry blossom because of their short lives and also used them as a representation of blood drops. It is a symbol of simplicity, spring, and innocence.

It's also a symbol of hope. The season of cherry blossoms corresponds to the calendar and fiscal years in Japan. This marks the start of new beginnings like a pupil's first day in school or a person's first day at work. The intensity and liveliness of the cherry blossom allows anyone to dream and hope for big things in the future and to be optimistic.

It's a symbol of humility too. The blooming period of cherry blossoms are short, leading to an instantaneous flourish and sudden death. In the Japanese culture, the flower serves as a reminder of mortality and humanity. It reminds people that the life of a human being can end anytime just like the flower. The cherry blossom exemplifies this human condition and makes people realize that life is short and that they should live it well.

I feel like a cherry blossom. I know that life can be delicate and vulnerable.

The Japanese words *wabi* and *sabi* express a complicated feeling for simple beauty, a loveliness that is all the more precious because nothing lasts. Yet this exquisite beauty is all worth it.

My feelings for Mashalany are *wabi* and *sabi*. Nevertheless, I have no fear of embracing the journey. As the ancient samurai wrote take the moments that please the aesthetic senses in a chaotic life. No armor needed only my intuitive awareness.

Mashalany processes the virtues of samurai—an absolute moral standard, one that transcends logic. What's right is right, and what's wrong is wrong. The difference between good and bad and between right and wrong are givens, not arguments subject to discussion or justification, and a man should know the difference. Character, prudence, intelligence, and dialectics are important. Intellectual superiority is his esteem. Mashalany chooses compassion over confrontation and benevolence over belligerence, and he demonstrates the ageless qualities of manliness. Love, magnanimity, affection for others, sympathy, and pity are the traits of benevolence—the highest attribute of the human soul.

Habibi

Habibi is an Arabic word used to describe someone you like or love, a word of endearment.

Young Middle Eastern men and women do not date unchaperoned. The single men and women avoid situations where they would or could be alone. In Saudi Arabia, when a man and woman are in a car alone together, authorities will pull them over to check to see if they are married, and if they aren't, they are arrested. They pray for Allah to bring the correct person for long-lasting marriage. Virginity is their whole life. The concept of an unmarried mother simply does not exist. Young people consult with family and friends in order to bring their true love to fruition. The young people are not allowed to be alone, and they don't look at each other, so there is little chance of physical attraction. The minds are able to meld together. Even kissing is not permitted until after marriage, lessening the chance for any premarital sex. The culture protects women with a high standard of modesty. Most of the women feel protected, respected, and secure because of these strict laws. The heart and soul are engaged first.

Habibi, you are near, even if I can't see you. You are with me, even if you are far away. You are in my heart, my thoughts, and my life always.

Habibi means being the loyalty needed, the consistency required, the passion craved, and the balance needed, all of which encompasses the love deserved.

This term of endearment means a lot to me, and the glory Mashalany has bestowed on me is genuine. I feel his reference is a prize of the highest value.

I want to be Mashalany's favorite book, waiting for him to say I make sense.

Power of Cultures

The Japanese are stoic. They endure hardships without showing emotions. They are hardworking, proud, yet humble. The Japanese maintain *wa*, which means harmony. Arabs are more dramatic, expressive, and emotional, and they feel some distain for the Western culture. The similarities between all these grounds include humanity, etiquette, virtue, order, and most of all, they demand respect.

Kimonos are distinct for the Japanese, and they are gaining back popularity. For example, in Kyoto, if you wear a kimono, you receive a discount on purchases, encouraging the wearing of kimonos. Art is another word for kimono. The sleeves will reveal whether you are married or single. Very wide sleeves are for single females. Kimonos are beautiful to wear, and they hide the imperfections of the body.

It is a privilege to be feminine and dress with dignity. Young females should embrace their inner charm and awaken chivalry in men so that they are treated with respect. There is nothing frumpy about accentuating your inner grace and beauty. At the same time, you can dress with dignity and beauty in artful attire.

Living in today's vulgar culture, you can acquire the power of modesty.

The burka, worn by many Middle Eastern females, is another form of beauty. The burka is worn in respect to Allah or God. There is little chance for judgment. You have the beauty of her soul and heart through her eyes and voice.

The virtue of modesty is a combination of qualities that pleases the intellect and moral sense.

The Middle East and Japan are similar. Both people share food at the table. The eaten food is not the same, of course; however the sharing is the same. "Sharing is caring," Mashalany, the Arab king of my heart and soul, says. The mealtimes for both cultures are reserved for celebrating the day, sharing information, finding solutions, and bonding. Manners are more apt to be used and learned. Lively conversations abound the table. Japanese and Arabs are proud of their munificence or great generosity. Several dishes are displayed, and both cultures expect guests to eat well. There are customary saying for good wishes too. Some say, "May your table always be like this." Others say, "Continued health and happiness."

Mashalany includes me with his family mealtime. His brothers, sisters-in-law, nephews, and mother are sharing together. The picture of their table setting and food is so inviting. Mashalany describes in detail each edible delight. I feel privileged to be included in his family ritual.

Shoes worn outside of the home are forbidden inside the home by both cultures. You never bring in the dirt and filth from outside. Shoes in both cultures are taken off prior to entering the home, and house shoes or stockings are worn indoors.

The Japanese word *yugen* means subtlety and grace, which are aesthetic norms for beautiful and tasteful things.

The Middle East and Far East share both virtue and civility, and these are instilled through an appreciation of the arts, an attitude that pervades the cultures.

Miyabi has a few different meanings. It can mean elegance or refinement or the rejection of vulgarity. Mashalany and I have polished our mannerisms of the highest grace with an awareness of the transience of the things around us. Like an unripe persimmon, the world can be full of sourness. Mashalany and I have *shibui*, a Japanese word for the beauty of the simple. Therefore, we do not share the world's astringent taste. There are no artificial ingredients to the world Mashalany and I have created. We have restraints for absolute shibui. At the same time, we have *iki* for a pure and unadulterated relationship. Our rapport is simple, sophisticated, original, and spontaneous. We have an appetite for life that is refined with a distinctive flair. We are a phenomenon. We began as Jo-ha-kyu. We began slowly and accelerated. The deep and mysterious ways of the heart and soul are profound. We have a type of *geido* or appreciation for tacit communication. Our *enso* (or complete circle) is our universe, which is enlightened and filled with strength, elegance, and absolute. Both of our cultures demand and practice politeness, and politics are inseparable and integrated.

Social Media for the Heart Soul

My heart and soul story begins with social media. As a business woman, I am engaged in many forms of social media for interaction and business attraction, but I'm not using these platforms as a dating service. I am networking on a daily basis, meeting new people from all over the world and within the United States. There is no better venue for learning, educating, and enriching than connecting on social media.

On this particular fall day, a profile appeared, and I was instantly struck in my heart. His eyes were like coffee without cream and sugar outlined in dark charcoal, yet his skin was the color of coffee with cream and sugar. I couldn't take my eyes off him. I kept staring, and I wanted to keep looking. He was so inviting. *Am I addicted to him?*

I can't explain my feeling at the time. He was a complete stranger, and he was from a country I had never visited. Intrigued, impressed, and curious, we connect virtually.

Our messages back and forth were all professional in nature. We learned about each other's businesses and daily lives. My fascination and my desire to know more about him grew. You see, he was a Muslim man in a country where women were covered from head to toe. I'm eager to know why he is interested in conversing with me.

We then moved from a professional social media platform to a more well-known, casual form of engagement. This is where you learn about a person's friends, likes, pleasures, passions, dreams. You learn the reality of that person. Is it only through face-to-face interaction? Or (as we know to be true) can it be through words and expression of passion and emotion? People express themselves differently to different people through different forms of media. Sometimes people can express their *real* self through words, through social media, through other things besides physical contact and physical expression.

Media is where publications are displayed. Being social is the sharing of images, ideas, and opinions. So social media is a gathering for social interaction to enable instant expression in a simple fashion.

Two hearts find each other on social media and beat joyfully as one, two souls with but a single thought. Mashalany has touched my soul more than my body. He is the master of my soul, and our hearts are a reflection. Love is the beauty and light of the soul. Mashalany doesn't care about my face. He knows the significance of my mind, heart, and most importantly, my soul. There is no need for words. There's a complete understanding. We are calm. There's no agitation, only peace.

Mashalany showers my soul with sunshine and smiles, which feeds my heart, and then my soul is restored. I do not need my lips. Mashalany's song engulfs the house of my soul.

Unlike romantic love, which feeds on pleasure and gratification, Mashalany allows receptivity for basic goodness—a powerful energy that emulates from his heart and soul. His motives and reasons are unfathomable for transcending time, worldly concerns, or place. We delight in our being. Our boundaries dissolve and flow into and surround our hearts. Romantic love is a fantasy bond through amorous words and gestures, which lack authenticity and vulnerability. Romantic love is usually short-lived and leaves each one longing for real love.

Middle East Meet Far East

This is where his name of authority is different from his realty. Mohammed is his professional name, and Mashalany is his other media name. I inquired why the different name. He kindly explained it was a nickname in Arabic that meant peach. My heart again was pierced because Momotaro means "peach boy" in Japanese. Awe and blood enters the heart and flows through. Momotaro enters and stays. I have liked many and loved so few. I would wait for hours just for one moment with Momotaro.

Mashalany in Arabic is peach, and Momotaro is a Japanese children's story about a peach boy. The Japanese folklore about the peach boy was found in a peach floating down the river. An old women who longed to have a child of her own found the peach and brought to back to her home. When her husband returned home, the wife exclaimed, "Look at this giant beautiful peach I found floating in the river. Let's cut it open for our dessert." When the husband started to cut open the peach, a cry came from the inside. The woman and man were astonished. They careful cut open the peach and found a baby inside. They baby was very well cared for and grew up to become a very well know samurai, the strongest and bravest in the land.

What could be romantic about a story about a peach? There will be another peach, more seasons, another smile, another tear, another year, but there will never be another Mashalany.

This peach from the Middle East has the same heart of Momotaro—strong, brave, kind, gentle, and appealing.

This peach from the Middle East and the Japanese Momotaro is like the forbidden fruit. He is sweet, full of flavor, tempting by the soft outer skin. This peach is a perfect peach. The temptation to touch is a struggle.

I am motivated to know more about Mashalany.

When you are unable to physically touch their hand or arm, you voluntarily use words for interaction. You become patient, kind, and generous. Jealousy is not acquired. "I trust you" is a better compliment because you can't trust the one you love; however, you can love the one you trust.

Technology allows for quick messages without the long wait of sending letters. However, messaging still necessitates the obligation of using words. Mashalany offers a source of inspiration and continual intellectual stimulation. My enthusiasm is childlike as my curiosity and inquisition begins. I want to know more about his daily life as a Muslim and professional life in the Middle East. I am fascinated by his life and he maintains his worship, vocation, and entertainment.

The Japanese will tell you they are not religious; however, they have a temple or shrine on almost every street corner. The Japanese show gratitude every day.

Both societies have much in common. They express respect and polite speech when addressing one another. Mealtime for both cultures is important and always in a shared environment. "Sharing is caring," to quote Mashalany once again. In today's world where work is valued above most things, family shared meals are not as common. However, in Japan and the Middle East, meals are important and expected part of each day. These meals are a celebration of the day for exchanging daily triumphs, talking about difficulties, and learning or sharing a good story or laugh.

Perhaps I believe in the mythology of Momotaro—the legend of strong in body and fierce when necessary. He is a protector and close family member with great morals.

Mashalany is gentle by nature, and he should be a proud Arabian. He brings out the best in me. He makes me feel as though I could grow wings and soar.

I marvel at the miracle of a blossoming rose. What would it feel like to be a blossoming rose? Love is not always perfect. The power of love for true happiness is complex as a rose completes full bloom. Everything leading up to the rose in full bloom is what makes the final beauty of the rose; not the instant formation of a rose.

Mashalany is like the owl, handsome and wise, or a ghost whose spirit never dies.

The anticipation of Mashalany taking my hand causes my heart to beat faster and the touch of my soul. My reality is finally better than my dreams. I wish we were butterflies for only three days, for in these three days, we would fill more than fifty years.

I can now imagine a kiss from Mashalany, and with it, I forget all of existence.

Seize of My Heart and Soul

There is no time or place with a heart and soul. It happens in a heartbeat, a single throbbing moment. It is like Mashalany slipped into my skin, invaded my blood, and seized my heart.

Love is not blind; however, it should be blind to the physical body. If all you had was the aptitude to see a person's heart, soul, and mind before the physical, you would acquire the solid foundation for a true partnership and long-lasting relationship. When you are engaged with the soul, sensitivity, power, and knowledge will trump any physical attraction. When you expose your soul, others will cherish your essence. They will strive to earn your respect and the purity of your heart. The physical body is only a vehicle for holding the essence of the soul and heart.

When you have acquired the heart of a man or woman, he or she will follow you anywhere. The lust of the heart and soul is the highest form of ecstasy. Opening up your soul and sharing your spirit, thoughts, fears, future, hopes, and dreams is the truest form of nakedness.

True love is only understood by the heart. The love in your heart lasts forever, but the physical changes. The heart and soul remain the same through life on earth.

Infatuation is fragile and will shatter when life becomes fragile. The heart and soul see all the flaws and blemishes. When you can see with the heart, you accept the habits and mannerisms of others. The heart recognizes fear and insecurities and comforts others. The heart works through challenges and painful moments.

The ability to be drawn into Mashalany through his heart and soul has been the most amazing involvement. I have lived behind his eyes and rested in the quiet shadows of his heart. All I need is the sanctuary of his heart.

Instant gratification and a culture that seemingly values monogamy less and less makes true love seem unobtainable. Are there good people left? Infatuation is masquerading as love.

Love is one of the strongest driving forces for humanity. We pursue it and crave it from family and friends. Love allows us to be attached to other human beings. We want to be the best version of ourselves.

Seduce my mind, and you have my body. Find my soul, and I'm yours forever.

My desire for Mashalany grows each day. I crave his voice. I long for a message from him. I just want to see his name. I am at the point that I am addicted to him. How is this possible? Only through my heart, mind, and soul.

With the mind, your body will discover the pleasures that were unknown before.

Mashalany has supplied courage and strength unsurpassed and essential to me merely with his mind. His soul is a mirror for my joy, amazement, and wisdom.

Pure untainted love from the neck up is iconic love.

A Trinity

Heart, soul, and eyes are the trinity of love. Each one is separable yet linked. I can feel everything with my heart and soul. My eyes are the door to open my heart. The physical is not needed when I open the eyes of my heart and I feel Mashalany's presence. There is no separation, no division, and no barriers. Our heart-to-heart, soul-to-soul dialogue has been a light in my life. You can't have one without the other. A relationship built on only one of these elements will most likely not survive. This is what platonic love is all about.

Benevolence is not only bringing joy to someone's life. Mashalany also has the desire to make me happy. He has complete understanding because of his depth. Mashalany has compassion and the ability to erase pain. Mashalany brings great joy with ease. His adeptness for equanimity is comforting. I have enough space around my heart and all around myself.

Mashalany consummates a relationship based on commitment without the infatuation or sexual desire. Passion penetrates my heart and soul like a fire.

Mashalany is patient and accepts me as who I am, not as who he wants me to be. He has complete understanding, appreciation, and devotion. Loyalty and devotion bring togetherness.

The passion of the body has an expiration date, but dedication lasts a lifetime. Mashalany has the companionate love that will last a long time. He offers me his devoted friendship and unrelenting respect. Mashalany's way promotes constantly learning new things and sharing new experiences, which creates excitement and commitment. The novelty will never wear off.

When you experience real love, you will not spend the rest of your life trading imitation love (sex, money, power, or ego), which leads to fear, emptiness, and unfulfilled relationships.

Mashalany cultivates my attention by pointing out my higher qualities, which is infinitely more rewarding and allows me to see more goodness in him. He does so by the guidance of his heart for continuing growth and appreciation. I am able to be my authentic self because our souls are complete. Mashalany has a loving and kind demeanor that flow with understanding. The heart and soul freely allows an unconditional relationship without repayment. It gives a sense of value that we treasure. In a world of expectations and reactions and the receiving end is astounding. This is a pure act of generosity. With your heart and soul revealed, you are able to see beauty all around—the birds singing, the cloud formations, music, reflections in the water, the smell of flowers, the skyline, the mountains, just to name a few. Mashalany provides a beacon of light guiding me to all areas of our relationship.

No Intrusions

Mashalany and I only have our conversation. No movies, no group of friends distracting our conversation. We learn to share our feelings, our emotions, and what is going on in our lives in a one-on-one environment. We do not have any physical distractions, and we survive by our emotional connections. We are forced to be clear in our words and the intention of our words, which we chose carefully. Like a blind person, we are unable to see if the other person is upset, angry, or stressed. We only have our honest feelings, and we are prepared to share.

Mashalany and I have a valuable appreciation for each other. We are unable to take each for granted. We are able to build bridges of appreciation, kindness, respect, and honor with our words. Even though we have some language barrier, he speaks, writes, and understands English; however, certain statements can cause confusion. The reward is to ask Mashalany to explain.

Thus, we have achieved a broad spectrum of clear and concise communication for understanding.

Language differences can be confusing when you are speaking or writing. Even though Mashalany has a good command of English and I know no words in Arabic, we clarify at times what is being conveyed. In addition, there are cultural barriers, gender barriers, physical barriers, and emotional barriers. The barriers are resolved easily with patience by asking questions, listening, and understanding the direction of our conversing. We cannot assume the words are understood. Mashalany has a delightful way. He always asks me, "Do you get me?" That is his way of ensuring we are on the same page of our thoughts. Most of the time, I do "get him," and when I do not understand, he easily explains his intentions. This is common in our interactions, and it feels natural for us.

Sometimes I am rewarded with a surprise "Good morning" from Mashalany. Even greater, sometimes I receive a sweet "Good night," which is totally unexpected. It's like he actually read my mind. His mind knew what my heart needed at that exact moment without prodding, without a hint.

Mashalany is a treasure. He thinks deeply. He is loyal, honest, and true; however, the simply things mean so much to him. His purity is what makes him.

Take this feeling and multiply it by infinity. Continue to the depths of forever, and you would still only have a glimpse.

Nobility in a Common World

Mashalany has true nobility and compassion, and he is not conceited. As a commoner, access into the world of privileges of heredity is found with Mashalany. He exudes the presence of a king with his words of respect, reason, direction, honor, and wisdom. Mashalany has made me feel like his queen. Together, we are able to reign.

We offer each other support for our dreams and goals. This is the process of building a solid foundation of openness, honesty, trust, support, loyalty, and devotion beyond jealously or self. We have built the basis for a cherished companionship.

I feel the true treasure of a person lies not in what can be seen but what cannot be seen. Real love lies not in what is done and known but in what is done but not known.

Pouneh Ordibehest said, "Women are made to think their body is an object and their face as a mask thus, she is in constant need of improvement, disguise, and alteration."

All women should be appreciated for their inner strength, intellect, and inner beauty—like the veiled women. I am like a veiled woman with Mashalany. He can't see me with his eyes. He can see my heart by my words and actions. Our heart and souls are in step, and we manifest our peaceful relationship. We both release paradigms from our hearts and souls for a graceful exchange. We are anchored in our hearts for a clear, radiant, concise, and empowering relationship—all veiled.

Heart and Soul

The heart can go on beating when the soul is in control. The heart is where impossibilities are attained.

Love doesn't need a reason. Pure love comes from the heart and soul without reason and stay.

This type of love and devotion awakens the soul and forces us to reach for more, which sets the heart on fire, and at the same time, it brings harmony.

With the heart, I have been able to see rightly what is essential and invisible to the eye of Mashalany. In order to make the right choices, you need your heart. With the guidance of only your heart and soul, few mistakes are possible.

The heart and soul are the seats of life and emotions. The heart and soul are blind. Therefore, only the beauty within is revealed. The heart and soul are the lights of beauty. We cannot see truly with our eyes. We have seized each other's hearts.

We have a powerful relationship and friendship because we have an appreciation for our similarities, and at the same time, we recognize and respect our differences. We don't seek what is outside of each other. We seek each other for the magnificence of inside.

Sometimes I am in agony because his other friends and family can see him and remain in his good company and I cannot.

He makes my heart race and my breathing turn shallow. I forget about the shell of my body, which separates the mingling of our souls.

Mashalany tells me I am a woman of valor and I am worth more than jewels. He trusts me, and I give him kindness of my tongue. I feel it is beautiful to experience our mysterious way, stand rapt in pure awe, and wonder about the enchantment we share.

Our hearts and souls are strengthened and empowered for perfection like our mothers' were. He is dearer to me than my than my soul. His words are like a song. My heart is in his lyre. In a hushed tone, he tells me I am more precious than Arabian jasmine. With confidence, he states I am a palm tree planted in his mind. Neither storm nor ax can fell it. He smashes all of my idols. He is my knight of all knights.

I would provide him water from my tears and add years to his life by giving him my own. I am the most faithful of heart. When will we be able to spend all our time together? My joy comes feeling life spring from his heart.

We are a work of art, miraculously in harmony, detached from time. He is the beginning of everything, and reality is now better than my dreams.

Mashalany did not whisper into my ears but into my heart. Mashalany did not kiss my lips but my soul.

Thoughtfulness

Being thoughtful is a lost art in today's society. Being thoughtful is being considerate and having regard for another person's desires. It means being helpful and not selfish. Being thoughtful simply means making a conscious decision for others. We pay attention to what is going on around us. We go out of our way to do something for someone else. Practicing thoughtfulness and helping another person only takes a moment. Thoughtfulness is stepping out. It is not complicated, and it welcomes kindness and compassion.

Mashalany processes extraordinary thoughtfulness. As a tourist in New York City for the first time, he visited an Arabian night club. This considerate man sent me a text telling me where he was and a recording of the music he was listening. I was so impressed, so touched because he took time away from his friends to include me. Not many men would include someone he only knows through social media. This is another example of the power of a heart and soul. The romance of his exceptional inclusion is a rare trait. Mashalany's actions are much louder than words, and so I have treasured them.

Sexy can be thoughtful, kind, considerate, patient, and generous. Outward appearances changes. The heart and soul of person is the sexiest part of a body. Indulge yourself, be complete, and be at peace, for you will experience the most incredible climax.

How does he know how to share these small yet important episodes with me? His heart is speaking. Our souls are bridged.

Another time he was at a comedy club with his friends. Once again, he sent me a recording of the comedians as a way of showing his desire to include me. We both laughed together. Sharing is caring. There is no need to be in his physical presence. This charitable involvement is all I need to have. I did not request to be part of his fun. His heart speaks to me. His subtle and gentle way is so invigorating, and he has my utmost gratitude. I feel privileged to be part of his company of friends even through social media. Mashalany's charisma is my anchor. These acts of kindness cannot be measured. You cannot put a price on them. His benevolence is as natural as taking a breath of air.

The soul knows the geography of our destiny. It is only with the heart that one can see rightly. What is essential is invisible to the eyes.

Self-perpetuating synergy-inspiration for being a better human-being, to do better, live better. This is the mystery of Mashalany and our heart and soul.

Be frugal with your short time on earth. Take this precious time to feel the heart so that the soul can lead you to magic.

When the heart and soul are engaged, there is no room for jealousy. Social media can be a graveyard of misunderstanding because of certain posts. Unnecessary jealousy allows the mind to create superfluous accusations. Mashalany alleviates these needless emotions. He provides an explanation for each posting that I might misinterpret. Mashalany has many female friends, and of course, they all share events. One time he was engaged in a contest determining who could run the farther, and he used social media to post the mileage. Mashalany assured me he was having fun with the competition. Another time while in he was Dubai, several of his female friends wanted to meet him. Once again, he assured me he would not be meeting them. He didn't have time to meet with them anyway. Mashalany has the gentleness of a great king. He provides sincere dedication and extraordinary trust. How could one not have full dedication? There is no room for question. Mashalany prevents any discord. I have absolute trust built on Mashalany's word only. This makes for a powerful bond. It's the security most needed in a true long-lasting relationship.

Mashalany has never seen snow before. I am enchanted with his colorful and mythological description when he discovered white snowflakes. We are chatting, and he portrays the theater of small creatures emerging on the snow in the quite of the evening. He sees a small rabbit and a squirrel. We are able to share the moment together. We both express our concern about the animals finding food and shelter in the cold. Through our heart and soul, we are communicating, sharing our concerns, expressing our sameness. We are not physically together, yet we are joined. Mashalany bestows his attention on me freely.

Each night as I go to bed, I hug my pillow and dream of Mashalany. Someday, I want to hug Mashalany and dream of my pillow.

You can believe in a love stored up for you like an inheritance. Have faith that this love has strength. This blessing is so large that you can travel as far as you wish without having to step outside of it.

I feel like my experience with Mashalany is ordinary in an extraordinary way. Our journey is eternal, not physical. Our celibate relationship is empowering. We have more time building a more meaningful and productive relationship. We have a deeply mindful and emotional connection. Sharing our emotions and feelings translates into understanding with agreement.

Mashalany sends me a concert with several musicians. We both can enjoy the music together and tell each other what we like and don't like about the music. He easily creates an atmosphere conducive to sharing without us being in the same place. We easily enjoy the music together.

Mashalany freely shares pictures of himself with friends while he's out enjoying a good restaurant or club. The activity is always full of joy, laughter, and delight. Again, I feel privileged to be included.

Mashalany frequently sends brainteasers for me to solve. So far I have been unable to solve one of the many he has shared. The solving is fun, educational, stimulating, and tricky. His way of testing my memory and brain skills are welcomed and challenging. Our interaction is balanced, and his generous advice is always appreciated when he stumps me. Part of his charm is teasing me with games. Mashalany has provided a virtual retreat for us from our everyday lives. These games he provides are romantic and creative for a typical relationship.

One day I received a picture of several shirts. He asked me to pick one because he was shopping. I was just so full of esteem. I wasn't next to him at the store, yet he asked for my humble opinion. We were shopping together.

Here's another way he embraces my assistance. He sent me two pictures of watches to help him select one for himself. The physicality means nothing to us. We are able to be with each other even if we are thousands of miles apart. I feel his aura.

Our relationship is dignified and composed. Even though we are miles apart, we can laugh together, play together, share meals together, and help solve problems, inclusion for our utopia.

Mashalany can engage me when ordering food. He has asked me what to order for takeout. He has involved me when he's at a restaurant. I can sense each flavor as he describes them.

I was able to speak with his nephews. They both speak English well. We had a lively discussion of their travels to the United States. They have been to more states than I have! What a pleasure to be able to speak with part of his family so easily and comfortably. We laughed together and shared many fun activities.

Our Own Universe

During the World Cup, we were miles apart, and we could still share the game. I wasn't able to watch one of the games, and he sent me exciting messages with the scores. All the while he was with his friends, yet he included me as one of his guests, ensuring I would not miss out. Mashalany and I create our own universe for special moments. Mashalany created a virtual seat for me at his table.

Our eyes see the strength of our souls, and our hearts have no limits.

Mashalany has his mind in two places at once. He is having a great time with his friends at one location with such grace his embracement has created sporting event for all us. This is not as easy as it may seem. His intellect has the ability to hold his attention for all of us to function for enjoyment. Men tend to do things together as opposed to women who are just together.

When we are in each other's dreams; we can always be together—no matter what happens.

No words from Mashalany are necessary. He is able to express himself and overcome the distance freely without tokens of professed love or reassurance, and I am able to feel his presence. I'm one of his closest friends, even though I am thousands of miles away. Everything seems simpler when we have continents between us. The separation can endure any circumstance, and we can reach our destinations.

The brightness from a star is immeasurable, and our relationship cannot be measured either. Our past and our future are irreverent.

Distance has the same effect on the mind as with the eyes.

The Heart Has True Eyes

Attunement of the heart and soul is communication. The heart is centered for direct communication and contact. You can feel it if something doesn't feel right. You may ask, "Is this worthwhile, or is it better to avoid this?"

Heart and harmony are synonymous. Heart stands for helpfulness, love, connection, and healing. The things you do with your heart and soul are completed with joy, love, and intense feelings.

Feelings are the language of the soul. They are enormously important for understanding your situation, where you are going, and what is good for you.

With the heart and soul in tune, you will live in the oasis of love and harmony. You will not lack confidence, be unsure, or have doubt. Surrendering the heart and soul allows for kindness, gentleness, tenderness, selflessness, generosity, peacefulness, empathy, compassion, and healing.

With heart and soul relationships you feel long-lasting intensity with more significance and value. Mashalany is so far away, but I can still feel him. The essence of his being is in everything I say and do. The nearness of his spirit takes my breath away. I feel him in every beat of my heart as I go throughout my day. When I close my eyes, I get such feelings of bliss. I can see Mashalany's gentle face and feel the fire in his caress. He tiptoes across my mind in the gentlest ways. Mashalany is in the softness of a rose and the warm wind on my face. Mashalany is the sunbeams from heaven shining brightly in my soul. He's in the sweetness of serenity that fills my heart. He will always reside inside my mind. Even though we are far apart, I can feel him with me, always tugging gently at my heart. With the sweetest devotion, I know he loves me too. We'll be together in spirit, and I'll forever love him.

Truly seeing is not done through the eyes. It is only accomplished through the heart.

Mashalany brings us equality by the gift of his heart. The physical world is full of differences and distinctions. Mashalany and I share congruence through our hearts, and we are radiant. Our hearts are not mere organs within our bodies. We see the world and ourselves differently. We are equals. Mashalany has rekindled my vision through his heart. I'm truly enlightened.

Mashalany has unleashed the hidden power of our hearts for coherence. His courtesies seem small and trivial, and they strike my appreciative and grateful heart. He doesn't need words. He articulates himself with the inaudible language of his heart. His heart has revealed the door of my soul, and he heals everything in sight.

Mashalany's leadership appeals to me because of his heart, not his mind. He appreciates the beauty of my heart, and lasting friendship will keep us forever young. He has sparked a heavenly fire in my heart, on that kindles up and beams light into the darkness of adversity. We have no diversity with our hearts joined.

True Devotion

The world is full of divorce and dysfunctional families. A husband or wife feel they are not fully committed. They are not sharing their full love, and there is distance between them. They are unavailable to each other. When you have multiple partners, you are sharing a bit of your soul with each partner. Eventually, when you have spread pieces of yourself around, your soul becomes empty. You are unfeeling. Be protective of your heart and soul. This bond will bring more joy and attract happiness into your life.

Mashalany takes my breath away when I see his picture. Beauty captures the eyes; personality apprehends the heart. Only a few have achieved love with the heart and soul. One soul inhabits two people, and *viola*, you have an authentic commitment.

Breathe into each other's hearts, and the hearts will beat as one.

The heart and soul provide profound guidance while the intellect serves a purpose. The intellect can fail to comprehend the complexities of situations. The intellect can't feel. Mashalany doesn't mask his feelings through his intellect. He is communicating through his intuition. Mashalany feels with his heart. Consequently, those actions speak louder than words. Mashalany does not have conditions. He does not talk without intention, and he does not give without reason. He cares without expectation.

Will we run out time? We need to live each moment as if it were our last. We must live in the moment and be present with each other.

Mashalany is the kind of goodness everyone needs in their lives before leaving this earth. He has awakened my soul, and I want more of the fire he has created in my heart.

In the virtual world, sending a message quickly and wishing someone well is gratifying.

People confuse sex with love. It's not the same, not even close. To be truly emotionally fit and mature, the heart and soul must be engaged. They must be in sync. The heart and soul connection sets you both free. It doesn't tie you both down. The physical world changes. The heart and soul remain unchanged. This devotion is so much more valuable. It's priceless.

A critical factor in any relationship is communication. Mashalany and I have other ways of communicating. Our words are accepted, and they are enchanting. They are the only aphrodisiac we need for fulfillment. If you only see the outside, then infatuation follows, and many times it all ends in failure. The heart and soul working in tandem can repair any damage with understanding, compassion, grace, and resolution.

Love in its nature is from only the heart and soul. We are connected internally. A true state of heart and soul is perfectly monogamous. Our subconscious is not continuously looking for true love and devotion because our hearts and souls are complete. Our complete openness makes us one. The magical powers illuminate and trigger the transformation and intention for bringing joy to each other. We have developed our spiritual dimensions for solid communion. We have no veil of secrecy.

All about the Peach

Momotaro is a Japanese legend. A baby found in a giant peach by a loving couple who desired all their lives to have a child of their own. This peach boy is secure and confident. He's a strong, powerful, obedient, and loyal defender. He's adventurous yet full of love. And he became a man of influence and honor. As mythical as Momotaro seems, his attributes are the solid foundation for any relationship, and he should be respected. The story is one of the most popular from Japanese folklore. Its theme—the unification of people separated by hostility—resonates throughout history, and it can be applied to many different cultures. Respect is a requirement in any solid, long-lasting relationship. Momotaro and Mashalany are a consolidation for wisdom and inspiration.

We all arrived on earth the exact same way. Each one of us was born with a heart and soul to deliver a different message.

Patience is a remarkable virtue that is reinforced by detachment. I cannot expect a quick response or a reply in my time frame. I must wait to see his name appear in a message.

At the same time, the anticipation is elevating.

Acceptance is another invaluable and necessary trait. Accept, appreciate, and acquire these essential traits. I must control my mind so I don't sling unwarranted accusations that I have conjured up in my own imagination.

Appreciation is exhibited and not neglected. Showing appreciation does require expression in a tangible form.

Mashalany is quite gifted at sending the appropriate music links. He sends these at just the right moment. It's like he reads my mind. Music is a gift that can last long and remain in the mind for years. The music can be enjoyed over and over again with no degradation. The melodies are fervid as I cherish the perfect choices each time. The songs Mashalany has selected are not common, which makes me treasure each tune. Mashalany is evocative.

We live in a world obsessed with love. It permeates our music, movies, novels, TV, and all of our entertainment. Most of this entertainment is based on pretend love. Our desire for love is within each breath we take. We all aspire to succeed in finding strong, long-lasting, deep, and forever love for each other. True love is not to be confused with puppy love. Do you really desire a dog's life? True love has brought more pain, diseases, destruction, and bitterness than any other quest. True love is not the same as sexual attraction and appetite. You cannot confuse sexual desire with love. Sex is an act, and love is a process. Sex is instinctive, but heart-and-soul love is learned.

Sex requires no effort. Heart-and-soul love needs time to grow, mature, and develop. Sex without love is boring and banal.

Mashalany gives, desires, and appreciates. He endures true romance from his heart and soul.

Loneliness can be reduced when your heart is engaged. The timbre of the heart will intensify, guiding our actions and intentions. The soul is awakened as we reach for more that sets our heart on fire and brings peace to our minds. Mashalany and I have now produced our own recipe for something rare and beautiful.

Prominence is where the heart and soul regulate and dominate. If your heart and soul are prominent together, they will prepare your path for any obstacle. Loyalty is power unchallenged.

Impeccable listening skills are mandatory. Mashalany and I tenderly pay attention to the minutiae of our voice and words. This is essential for comprehension. I can't see his facial expressions or body language. I only have access to his voice and texting. We rely on the inflection of our voice and our laughter. I don't need to see his body. I can feel his spirit penetrate my soul and heart. Each verbal utterance is euphony. His words are whispered to my heart, and they kiss my soul.

Distance means so little when someone means so much. Each of us is comfortable with who we are. Mashalany is much more outgoing, and he appreciates the companionship of his friends on a regular basis. He does have a serious side when it comes to his work, and he's earning his MBA in international business. He is well achieved and recognized all over the Middle East. I am not so keen on being out and being seen. I enjoy my own company and learning about other people.

Mashalany is not bathetic. He commands the power of his words as a king would with a softness. With his words, he is very confident and doesn't let any opinion interfere with his focus.

Proud to be a Woman

I am a good woman. I can look like that slightly frazzled girl in the mirror when I know I am going to be late getting out the door.

As a good woman, I am the greatest balancing act of all time. I have a little bit of spice along with the sweetest intentions. I am not the nicest. Nor am I the meanest. I am my best friend's emergency phone call at 4:00 a.m. and my mother's lifelong shopping companion. I am not perfect, but I know I am perfect for myself.

I make mistakes, which means I am trying. I get knocked down. I don't always have the best luck all the time. I overanalyze things. I can be a true mess of emotions, yet I am human. I also know that persistence pays off, that the worst people can tell me is no, that if you dream it, it honestly can happen, and that surrounding myself with optimism is key. I am goal-oriented and independent. I don't mind company. In fact, I love company.

I love a good man. I know a good one when I see him. I believe that giving is far greater than getting, that patience is exactly what I thought it would be—a virtue. And I believe that the perfect relationship doesn't exist. There's just the perfect balance. I cherish my friends and adore my family, and I'm smitten until old age by that certain someone. I am young at heart and old-fashioned by nature.

I celebrate life. I celebrate everything in it—the birthdays, the losses, the milestones, the setbacks, the whole journey. I keep God in my life. I turn to him, hide from him, run to him, and trust in him. I know anything is possible with him because I am a reflection of him. I relish in all possibilities of life.

I walk with confidence and tousled hair, and I tell witty jokes. I have a glowing smile and a contagious laugh, and positive energy abounds. That is where I am and exist.

I feel deeply and love passionately. My tears flow as profusely as my laughter. I am both soft and powerful and both spiritual and practical. I aspire to be a gift to Mashalany and the world.

Gifted Teacher

Mashalany is gifted as a teacher of his Muslim practice. He has a tender way of explaining each requirement. He's devout with the love of his family traditions. There are two holidays of Islam, Eid Al-Fitr and Eid Al-Adha. Eid Al-Fitr is celebrated at the end of Ramadan (a month of fasting), and Muslims usually give *zakat* (charity) on occasion. Eid Al-Adha is celebrated on the tenth day of Dhu al-Hijjahand, and it lasts for four days, during which Muslims usually sacrifice a sheep and distribute its meat among family, friends, and the poor. Mashalany spent Eid Al-Adha with his cousin. He shared with me the wonderful time he had and the joyous celebration. His cousin is a farmer, and they barbecued a lamb. It looked delicious. Mashalany said it was one of his best celebrations. The picture he sent indicated he has a great gene pool. His brothers and cousin are very handsome indeed. He also shared a picture of his father. Mashalany greatly resembles him—tall, dark, and handsome like *GQ* men. Yet he is not conceited about his physique or good looks.

A soulful love relationship is built on transparency. It is about the countless feelings and emotions shared. It's about complete trust.

The soul is supported by wisdom and knowledge. The soul is pure energy for tranquility and purity. The heart is encouraging of the pursuits of the soul. The heart is like a filter for compassion, caring, and commitment. Together the heart and soul will take pure compassion and love to a whole new level. With the energy from the heart and soul, there is little need from your mind. With the heart and soul, there is simplicity, and it will manifest your complete purpose. The chemistry of the heart and soul will allow two people to soar through a love of the upmost magnitude.

Since the heart and soul are inaudible; domination over the mind for the most beautiful words made audible. The hegemony will be the change for gracious relations. Souls recognize each other by vibes, not by appearances.

Intimacy is not purely physical. It is the art of connecting with someone so deeply that you can see into that person's soul.

Love is something that knows no measure. We cannot put it together with our minds. It cannot be cultivated. It is not sentimental. When you acquire true love through the heart and soul, there is no room for the mind to make up jealous, deceitful, and angry thoughts.

With this love, there is no duty or responsibility. Love is not about jealousy because jealousy is about the past and love is active in the present. Love does not obey. Love is not a habit. Habits are boring and destroy freedom.

There is nothing more alluring than actually seeing someone's soul through their eyes. The experience of being lost in Mashalany's eyes is begging to find out more. There is nothing more mysterious behind those eyes that does not solicit the discovery of his universe. Yet there is limited time for exploration in this lifetime. I want to retreat to his eyes for calmness and deep thinking. There is no escaping those eyes because the eyes change the very essence of who I am. When walking through his eyes, I can walk in Mashalany's shoes, and they become my shoes. I can feel the empathy. I have the same joy, love, and fears. The vision is the same for both. I feel lost. Nevertheless, I want to stay lost. I forget how to breathe, how to talk, how to walk, and how to dance. I'm completely transcended into one world, and I feel amazing, confident, and stupendous. To see his soul through his magnificent eyes is mesmerizing. I can actually see why and how he acts.

Through Mashalany's eyes, I can see the horizons of infinity. I can truly connect with him. The heart wants what the heart wants. His eyes are so captivating that I'm lost forever in them. I'm not fearful. It is tantalizing, explorative, vast, and exciting. I am enriched with intellectual stimulation not found in the physical sense.

I want to be the smile on his lips.

When your heart and soul are connected, you will have a lifetime companion. Mashalany is not a romantic partner. He is a great friend. A soulmate is a kindred spirit, a reflection of another person. Even though there is distance between us, we are connected. Souls don't know age or time, for the soul is as old as the universe. A soul mate will motivate you to discover yourself. A true soul connection is rare and needs patience and perseverance. It's well worth the time. The seduction of the soul and heart is the ultimate experience, and it is not known to many. The pull of the soul is so strong you can control it or stop it. With Momotaro, my dream is fulfilled, and I melt into his soul. We strengthen each other and speak to one another in silent, unspeakable memories. The soul keeps inspiring for eternity. A soul mate is like a mirror. He or she makes you a better person. Our physical bodies are just housing for our beautiful souls. Our love is friendship on fire.

He lives in my heart, and he is in my prayers.

One Day When Heaven Calls

One of my favorites songs Mashalany sent me one late evening is title "One Day When Heaven Calls". Music sometimes says what cannot be expressed, and it can often soothe my mind. Music is a gift from heaven and flows directly to the heart. The music Mashalany sends me makes me feel like he is talking to me with words he cannot say to me directly. He is telling me to dream without fears or limitations. He's like this song I can't get out of my head.

> I can see moon and light.
> Be patient, and forget all your sorrows.
> I see a bright future for you.
> I am still taking care of you.
> Although I am far from you,
> One day I'm going to fly away. One day when heaven calls my name,

I lie down and close my eyes at night.

If I had never met Mashalany, I could have dreamed him into being. His music is like what his feelings sound like.

I can feel the moon and light because I don't need my eyes to see. I can feel him. When that day arrives, I want to fly away. Heaven must be like his first kiss, and I will finally see his eyes when our estrangement ends.

Music has no language barriers. We can both understand entirely.

Mashalany said to me, "Fill your evening with music and the cares that invade the day shall fold their tents like the Arabs and silently move away."

For us music is as essential as the language. It is literature for our souls so that we can understand and express feelings and thoughts. It starts where our speech ends. Mashalany sends music that melds our soul together.

Is it possible to be in love? I hope it is not too late. It is like trying to count the stars. I can try, but it's impossible. The art of actually reading each other's heart and knowing what is hidden in our hearts completes us. The mere sound of his voice makes me joyful. He taught me patience and strength with no conditions.

We can hug in our thoughts. We can feel each other's breath because our souls are intertwined. I don't need to hear his voice. I am never lonely or lost. He is with me in spirit and mind. Thinking of him keeps me awake. Dreaming of him keeps us asunder. And that keeps me alive. These feelings can't be contained. They come from my fairy-tale dream.

I can't feel his heartbeat, yet I can feel the light shining from his heart and reaching out to mine. It is the most beautiful place on earth. I would cut my heart into a thousand pieces to form a constellation that could light his way to my heart. Our fate is set, and nothing can block the way.

Perhaps if I send my voice into the stars, the echo will be written in the clouds for him. You see, there is no separation when the heart and soul are connected. His soul swims through me and chimes in my bones. We can walk among the clouds together. It's as though he is the open sky and I am a bird flying.

We have opened our hearts, and we felt our souls merge. The infinity of stars has aligned through the portal of our soul and has united in our hearts.

Mashalany's music provides the moonlight to my gloomy night. He illustrates through sharing music. The mind has vast limitations; however, through the heart and soul, you are limitless and unconditional. The mind complicates and confuses everything. Together we have true aspirations from our hearts. Our souls have infinite peace, harmony, and bliss. Mashalany provides the nourishment needed for my heart and soul.

The sounds from human speech don't provide chills and thrills. Striped of their meaning, they don't inspire. The music he provides, however, touches my heart and soul. He has led me to his heart and soul. He has taken me.

I am not blinded by the picture of his physical body. He has brought focus and balance by leaving out the ego of his mind. I have a sense that I am complete without any comparisons. I feel lost in the amazement of his friendship. His music cleanses my understanding for constant inspiration, and it lifts us into a realm that we would not reach otherwise.

Although our worlds are different, we don't care because our feelings are transcendent.

Dance in the Rain

Mashalany doesn't have to say anything to me. He speaks directly to my heart. There is no miscommunication when the mind speaks to the heart. You need your feet to dance; however, dancing with two hearts is quite another feat. Our hearts are not dancing to impress anyone because no one else is judging. Our hearts are creating our own poetry, our own music. Our heart dance is the hidden language of our souls. If only the world could see the beauty of our hearts dancing.

Our hearts are familiar as one, no matter the circumstances or distance between us. The oneness of our hearts illuminates our powerful bond and gives birth to a new sense of humanity. Our souls are the fidelity for honesty and openness. We don't have the gratification of seeing our body language. We use our ears for listening to a cosmic intellect. Together we created a true revolution and paradigm shift in joining our hearts and souls to achieve an entirely new level of love.

Through the resonance of our heart and soul, we have the intensity for perfect communication. We have made a pathway of intimate, personal, and spiritual truth for a sacred heart-to-heart communion. We do not have a poverty of communication or deep listening. Our perfect communication leads to a telepathy, deepening of our oneness.

If we had physical encounters, we would not have the intensity or the meaningfulness of our soul relationship. Our souls did not come together to harm one another. We are united to further our learning at the level of our heart and soul. Our connection brings a different dimension and progression of the physical. The music of our souls radiates throughout the universe. The normal eye sees only the outside of a person. Our eyes pierce through the outside, reading and understanding each other's hearts and souls, finding areas that the outside could never detect. We liberate each other. We understand that which our minds cannot. The beauty within us is the reflection of our magic.

I believe Mashalany would bring me a star from the night sky if I requested one.

How I love the rain. I always wanted to dance in the rain. I once asked Mashalany if he would dance in the rain with me if we met in person. He said he would be delighted. He asked, "Will you take care of me if I get sick?" Of course, I said I would until he requested my departure. He replied, "Never." How can he make me feel this way with love as soft as a misty rain that gently touches my soul? This love is like a misty rain, falling softly, yet we are flooding our hearts.

I humbly pray that I shower him with the same affection. I want my love to rain down on him so thoroughly that he can't escape it. I'm going to keep showering him with it. I want it to sprinkle on his heart and soul forever. I want him to taste my thought process while I read. I want him to unravel my riddles with his tongue.

My mind is not caught up in the boundaries of a physical life, the drama and fears that abound. I will not be held captive. We bring out our true essence and wisdom emulating outward.

Our hearts are not subjected to the chaos or limited by pain, fear, or neurosis. We are creative, joyful, and respectful. We are heart thinkers, not head thinkers, which infuses our relationship with infinite compassion. We took the initiative with a seemingly illogical connection, which some would frown upon, even though it was the best heart decision. My heart is queen, and his heart is king. Together we rule. Our minds are our advisors; however, we see the bigger picture, and we are aware of our needs. We have the heart power for great riches and resources, which cannot be squandered or lost.

Who needs shelter from something this wonderful? I want to stay caught up in the storm of love, passion, and desire, bundled in a relationship that contains happiness beyond anything ever imagined.

Let it rain. Let it rain. Let it rain. I'll stay drenched.

I would rather have one touch of his hand and one kiss from his lips than an eternity without.

When I close my eyes, I am not afraid of the world. I want him to take my heart and run away. He is my denouement.

The best love is the kind that awakens the soul, that makes us reach for more, that plants the fire in our hearts and brings peace to our minds.

Mashalany has always been in my dreams. Is it possible to awaken to a fairy tale that has come true? My Arabian king has opened my eyes.

Mashalany is like a key that fits my lock. I feel he can unlock my paradise.

With Mashalany, I feel profoundly connected. It's as though the communication that takes place between us is not intentional but by divine grace. He completes me. He makes each moment magical. He brings out the best in me. I desire to be a better person, and I would drop everything, no matter the circumstances, to be there for Mashalany. He has created a heaven for me, which makes me his angel.

We are separated by thousands of miles, yet our affection makes me feel as if he were right next to me. We are in the same beautiful world we created together.

I can feel my soul leave my body and cross into another universe where time is a memory with Mashalany. He is like the best music in the world. He is the harmony of a thousand of his smiles. He illuminates our universe with a celestial expression of love that brightens the sky above as we soar into the infinite and heaven embraces us.

We are the story of how the sun loved the full moon the color of honey so much he died each night to let me breathe. Mashalany is the light that holds my soul, and he is my sun, my moon, and all my stars.

Our love is deep within us. We are epic.

His eyelashes touch my eyelashes for the first time as our eyes grow closer like butterfly wings, and our lips touch for the first time. The softness like the fuzzy soft peach skin and the warmth of his embrace is so strong and comforting.

Mashalany kissed me with such desperation it felt like he was drowning and I was his air. And then we smiled. He looked at me like I was more beautiful than a blossoming rose. I never wanted another pair of lips to touch mine as much as his.

If I could be anything in the world, I would want to be his teardrop. Because I would be born in his eyes, live on his cheeks, and die on his lips.

My heart belongs to no other soul.

The Arab king of my heart and soul completes me.

About the Author

Yuriko Terasaka is proud of her Japanese heritage. Traveling to Japan to visit relatives and embracing the beauty of Japan has been a journey of passion and devotion. She feels immensely blessed to have the privilege of being born from a Japanese mother and an American Indian father. Both cultures have enriched her perspective of life on earth. Her first book, *The Arab King of My Heart and Soul*, is a reflection of her desire for understanding the beauty of cultures around the world. At the same time, she desires to experience true romance.

The Tale of Genji is like *War and Peace*, both long reading yet necessary for acceptance, compassion, and good insight or judgment. Yuriko also can relate to some of the women in *The Tale of Genji*. She has enjoyed writing this first book because it is written entirely from her heart.

Aristotle considered the heart as the seat of thought, emotion, and reason. It is only with the heart you can see rightly and justly. What is essential is often invisible to the eye.

Yuriko genuinely wishes everyone to enjoy, learn, and experience a true love life on earth. She has sincerely enjoyed writing each word and sharing her experience, and she welcomes your feedback. Yuriko hopes you will share her book with friends and family for enlightenment and a different way of looking at true love of the heart, Little by little, we can open our eyes and go deeper than the physical. We can be role models, the exceptions. We can be different. We can be examples.

She loves traveling, walking, swimming, reading, most recently dragon boating or anything new that challenges her fear.

True love has no culture, boundaries, race, or religion. It is pure and beautiful like the moon's reflection on a quiet lake. To have the immortal essence to my being—is that *The Arab King of My Heart and Soul*?

Printed in the United States
By Bookmasters